DISNEY'S WORLD OF ADVENTURE

presents

THE UNDERWATER ADVENTURE BOOK

Random House 🏠 New York

CONTENTS

20,000 Leagues Under the Sea	7
Man-Eaters!	36
Diving for Treasure	39
Ocean Scientist	44
Nessie, Nessie, Come Out If You Are	49
The Loch Ness Mystery	54

Photograph Credits: Academy of Applied Sciences, 52; Tom McHugh/Steinhart Aquarium/PR, 36; V. Newbalt/Globe Photos, 37; Ron and Valerie Taylor/Bruce Coleman Inc., 38; Wide World Photos, 49.

Library of Congress Cataloging in Publication Data
Main entry under title: Disney's world of adventure presents The underwater adventure book. (Disney's world of adventure) SUMMARY: Includes an adaptation of the film "20,000 Leagues under the Sea"; articles on sharks, the Loch Ness monster, diving for treasure; and instructions for simple water experiments. 1. Sharks—Juvenile literature. 2. Loch Ness monster—Juvenile literature. 3. Diving, Submarine—Juvenile literature. [1. Sea stories. 2. Sharks. 3. Loch Ness monster. 4. Diving, Submarine. 5. Water—Experiments.] I. Disney (Walt) Productions. II. Series. [PZ7.D626 1978] Fic 77-90198 ISBN 0-394-83602-2 ISBN 0-394-93602-7 lib. bdg.
Manufactured in the United States of America   1 2 3 4 5 6 7 8 9 0

20,000 Leagues Under the Sea

The Sea Monster

IN THE SUMMER of 1866, a United States warship sailed southwest from San Francisco, California. She was the warship *Abraham Lincoln,* commanded by Captain Farragut. His orders were to find and destroy a deadly sea monster that had sunk dozens of ships in the southern Pacific Ocean. The beast was said to glow in the dark and to be larger and faster than any fish or whale known to man.

The ship carried her American crew and two French passengers: Professor Pierre Aronnax, of the Paris National Museum, and Conseil, his helper. Aronnax, a tall man with black hair and a pointed beard, was a scientist. He was famous for being an expert on the sea and its mysteries. Conseil, a short, plump young man with large, popping eyes, was his student.

Captain Farragut's plan was to divide the South Pacific into squares and to search the entire area of each square. For many months the ship sailed through the lonely waters, crossing and recrossing her path. But there was no sign of the beast she was hunting.

During all those endless days and nights, the most eager and watchful man on the ship was Ned Land, a Yankee sailor. Ned was known as the best whale-hunter in the business. He was a strong young man with a square jaw and a twinkling eye. Ned hoped to kill the monster with one throw of his harpoon. He kept this sharp, spearlike weapon ready at all times.

One night in December, Ned was on deck singing to a group of sailors.

Plunking his guitar, he began his favorite whaling song:

Got a whale of a tale
    to tell ya, lads,
  A whale of a tale or two,
'Bout the flappin' fish
    an' the girls I've loved,
On nights like this
    with the moon above,
A whale of a tale
    an' it's really true,
  I swear by my tattoo.

Professor Aronnax and Conseil joined the group of amused listeners. Ned grinned at them and continued his song:

There was Harpoon Hannah,
  With a face that made you
      shudder,
Nose like a banana,
  An' a chin just like a rudder...

His song was cut short by the booming voice of the ship's lookout, high in the crow's nest. "Ahoy! Burning ship off the starboard bow!" Captain Farragut ordered all hands on deck and steered toward the burning boat. But only minutes later the ship exploded and sank, shooting smoke and flame into the night sky.

"A terrible sight!" cried the

8

Chief Gunner's Mate. "She must have gone down with all hands!"

"Poor devils," said Aronnax. "What could have caused such a terrible explosion?"

"Gunpowder!" said the Chief. "A whole shipload of the stuff."

"But what could have set it off?" Ned Land asked. "She must have struck somethin'."

Aronnax shook his head. "It is possible, Ned, that something struck *her*."

The lookout suddenly called down again. "Ahoy! Shining object off the starboard quarter!"

Jerking their heads around, the men saw two gleaming spots like fiery eyes in the distance. They were moving fast just below the surface of the water.

"It's the monster!" Conseil cried.

"Gun crews to battle stations!" shouted the Chief. "Look sharp!" The men jumped to their places behind the guns. "Set your sights at close range—and FIRE!"

The big guns fired at the target but failed to make a hit. The monster was speeding in bright circles. Suddenly it turned sharply and came at the warship.

Yelling with excitement, Ned Land hurled his harpoon. It hit the monster but did no damage. An instant later the monster rammed the ship, smashing the rudder and throwing hatch covers and other things into the water. The crash knocked both Ned and Aronnax overboard. Seeing Aronnax in danger, the faithful Conseil jumped into the water to save him.

All night the three men hung on to a floating hatch cover, hoping to be rescued. But the warship, out of control and tilting to one side, drifted away. At dawn there was no sign of it. Just when the men were sure they would drown, they felt

themselves being raised upward.

"We're on the back of the monster!" Conseil shouted.

"But this is no monster!" cried Aronnax. "It is a submarine boat!"

"And made of iron," said Ned. "No wonder my harpoon bounced off her hide!"

"Men have long dreamed of boats that glide beneath the sea," said Aronnax. "But their dreams have never come true—until now. Here, at last, is a real undersea boat —a true miracle!"

"I can hardly believe it," said Conseil, his big eyes popping.

Aronnax called down through a hatch that had mysteriously opened. "Hello! Is anyone down there?"

"Don't hear a sound," said Ned.

"Then let's go down the ladder and have a look."

"Why don't we wait, Professor?" said Conseil nervously. "We might be asking for trouble."

"No, this craft might dive under the water and leave us to drown. Come on—follow me."

At the foot of the ladder the men found themselves in a chartroom.

It was as bright as day, although there was no sign of the usual oil lamps or candles. Walking ahead slowly, they entered a long salon with handsome furniture and thick carpets. Fine works of art hung on the walls. At the far end was a giant pipe organ.

Aronnax gasped. "There is great genius behind all this."

"And great evil," added Conseil. "Don't forget, Professor—this submarine must have sunk all those ships."

As they looked about in amazement, a black-bearded man in a captain's uniform appeared and spoke harshly.

"You are from the warship that attacked my boat, are you not?"

"Yes," replied Aronnax, "but we thought that this was a monster, not a man-made craft. I am Professor Pierre Aronnax and my companions are Conseil, my student, and Ned Land, master harpooner."

The Captain's eyes widened with interest. "I've heard of you, Professor, and studied your writings about the sea. I am Captain Nemo and my submarine is called the *Nautilus*."

"Thank you for saving us, Captain Nemo," said Aronnax. "If you had not lifted us from the water, we would have drowned."

Nemo grunted. "I want none of your thanks. You are my prisoners. And now that you know my secret— that your so-called monster is really an undersea boat—you must realize that I can never let you go free."

"Now wait a minute!" Ned Land said angrily. "You can't—"

"Be quiet!" thundered Nemo. "Or I will have you thrown back into the sea!"

Through a speaking-tube, he gave orders for the boat to dive and get under way.

Nemo rang a bell. "One of my men will give you dry clothing. You will change and join me for dinner in an hour."

Sunken Treasure

At dinnertime Captain Nemo seated himself at the table in the beautifully decorated dining room. While he was waiting for his guests, his pet seal came in. Barking for attention, she waddled over to the table. Nemo tossed her a few bits of food, which she gulped down in a flash.

"That's all, Esmeralda," he said. "Give me a kiss." He leaned down and received a wet smack on the cheek. "Good girl. Off you go now. I hear my guests arriving."

A sailor led Aronnax, Conseil, and Ned into the room.

"Be seated, please," Nemo said politely. "Your clothes are being dried and will be returned to you later. In the meantime, make yourselves comfortable."

Ned winked at Conseil. "Comfortable is right." To Nemo he added, "You do pretty darn well for yourself here, matey."

"You may address me as Captain Nemo," his host said coldly.

Served by one of the crewmen, the hungry visitors began to eat. When they were halfway through the meal, Conseil said, "The food is delicious, isn't it, Professor?"

"Excellent," Aronnax replied. "I have never tasted better. May I ask how you are able to serve such food as this, Captain?"

"These dishes all come from the ocean. There is nothing on this table that grows ashore."

"Remarkable. This meat tastes like veal."

"The flavor fooled you, Professor. It is fillet of sea snake."

Conseil quickly took a piece of food from his mouth. "Then—what I have here on my plate, Captain. I—uh—suppose it isn't lamb then?"

"No, young man, it's brisket of blowfish. The dressing is sea squirt with barnacle sauce."

Aronnax tasted a piece. "Mm, very good."

Nemo handed Ned a silver tray. "These are fruits made from sea cucumbers."

Ned made a sick face and said, "Not for me, thanks."

Aronnax took a bite. "I never would have guessed it. These fruits are excellent."

Nemo turned to Ned. "That's pudding you're being served. It's made from unborn octopus. Do taste it."

"Not me," said Ned roughly. "You've got nothin' here that's fit to eat."

"I agree," Conseil muttered.

"Well," said Nemo, "since we are nearing the sunken island of Crespo, you will have a chance to choose your own food."

Ned brightened. "Ya mean—we're gettin' off this boat?"

"Yes, for a quick underwater hunting trip." Nemo snapped his fingers and a sailor appeared. "Prepare Mr. Land and Mr. Conseil for a walk on the ocean floor."

When the surprised pair had been led away, Nemo offered Aronnax a cigar made of seaweed. The Professor smoked it with enjoyment. "You lead a civilized life here under the sea," he said.

Nemo's face darkened. "But I am not what is called a civilized man, Professor. I have finished with the world—so I do not obey its laws. But you will not be bored here. There are my books and paintings to enjoy, my collections of sea creatures—even music." He stood up. "But come—I'm sure you would like to explore my boat."

Leading the way, Nemo explained the workings of the *Nautilus*. "All of our heat, light, and motion come from electricity."

"But this is marvelous!" said Aronnax. "Scientists have dreamed of putting electricity to practical use! How did you do it? And how do you get electricity here under the sea?"

Nemo smiled and said, "From a special power source. You will see it later."

Taking the amazed Aronnax into the salon, he opened a large glass viewport and showed him the undersea garden outside. Lacy red sea fans and colorful groups of corals

waved to and fro. Golden butterfly fish and countless other bright creatures swam by.

"This is the sunken island of Crespo, Professor," Nemo said. "We do our hunting and farming here."

"All under water?"

"Yes, the sea gives us everything we need."

Men in diving suits now appeared outside the submarine. "They are my food collectors," Nemo explained. "The pair trying to keep up with them in the rear are Conseil and Land. Would you care to join them, Professor?"

"Indeed, yes. I would like to meet the wonders of the sea face to face."

In the diving chamber, Aronnax and Nemo were helped into special suits. Then they dropped onto the sea floor through the escape hatch.

It was a strange, twilight world that Aronnax entered. He felt as if he were setting foot on another planet. An octopus swam in for a close look at him and Nemo, then glided away. Just ahead, the food collectors were filling their baskets with sea ferns, lobsters, and turtles.

No one noticed that Ned and Conseil had wandered away from the group. Ned had spied a sunken ship and waved to Conseil to follow him. Together they entered the ancient wreck through an opening in its rotted timbers.

In the hold they came upon a large chest and excitedly broke open its rusted lock. Throwing back the lid, they found a treasure of jewels, rings, and gold coins. The two men looked at each other. Their eyes gleamed through the faceplates of their helmets. They picked up the heavy chest and carried it back out to the sea floor.

Suddenly Conseil dropped his end of the chest and pointed upward. A giant shark had seen them and was closing in quickly! Letting the chest go, Ned raised an arm to protect his head from the jaws of the killer. Both men fell flat. The

14

shark circled them once, then darted in for the kill.

But the shark never reached them. It was suddenly jerked aside roughly, to sink dead at Ned's feet. Captain Nemo appeared from behind a forest of ferns. In one hand he carried a gun, which had fired a death-dealing spear at the shark.

Nemo grasped Ned's arm and started to lead him away. Ned pulled back, pointing to the treasure chest. Nemo ignored it. He dragged Ned back to the *Nautilus,* leaving Conseil to follow.

After Ned had gotten out of his diving gear, he began to rage at Nemo. "You robbed us of a fortune! We left a treasure out there— a whole chest full of gold, silver, and diamonds!"

"We went out to get food, not treasure," Nemo said angrily. "Aboard the *Nautilus* we use trinkets like those as weights to keep the boat steady. Let me show you." Leading Ned to a vault in another room, he pointed to shelves piled high with jewels and gold bars. "You try my patience, Mr. Land," he said. "Rather than watch your every move, I could easily leave you out there in the sea with the chest you seem to value so highly."

Ned turned away, muttering, and walked back to the cabin he shared with Conseil. The little student and Aronnax were waiting there.

"Ned," the Professor said, "if you keep upsetting Captain Nemo, you will get us all killed. Now we must all be calm and stay together. It is our only chance to learn Nemo's secrets—and possibly to escape. Ned, promise me you will not start anything on your own."

"I won't promise that, Professor. I already have a plan to get free."

"Well, at least try my way first. I know I can win the Captain's friendship but I need time, and your help. Can I count on you?"

"Well—all right. I won't try any one-man battle—yet. But there's one thing you oughta know—Nemo's crazy. You can't make a deal with a mad dog. So while you're feedin' him sugar, I'll be figurin' out a way to muzzle him."

Aronnax and Conseil walked out, leaving Ned dreaming of Nemo's treasure.

Captain Nemo's Secret

During the weeks and months that followed, Aronnax passed the time by keeping a daily journal. In it he wrote about life in the *Nautilus.*

One morning Nemo took him to see the most secret part of the submarine—the power room. There each man put on a helmet with thick, dark glass to protect the eyes. Then Nemo opened a tiny door into a sort of furnace. A stabbing, blinding light leaped out at them. When the door had closed, Aronnax felt himself shaking.

"Captain Nemo, you have discovered the greatest source of energy in the world!"

Nemo nodded. "You are right. I have captured the secret power of the universe! And that power makes me master of the sea!"

"I can hardly believe it, Captain. How could one design and build such a craft as this? And control power beyond the wildest dreams of science? Such a secret could help the whole world!"

Nemo clenched his fists. "Or *destroy* it, Professor! Power can be used for evil as well as good!"

The two men walked in silence back to the salon, where Nemo pressed the lever that opened the viewport. They stood side by side, watching the strange undersea world gliding by.

"See how peaceful it is here," Nemo murmured at last. "The sea is everything. A huge world where

I roam at will."

He went on in a low voice, as if in a dream. "Think of it. Up on the surface there is hunger and fear. Men fight and kill one another. But here beneath the waves they have no power. Their evil drowns. Here, on the ocean floor, is the only independence. Here I am *free!*" He faced the Professor. "Imagine what would happen if evil men controlled machines like this submarine of mine. Far better that they think this is a monster and hunt me with harpoons."

Time went by. The *Nautilus* traveled 10,000 leagues under the sea—about 30,000 miles. Aronnax had still not learned the reason for Captain Nemo's anger toward mankind. But then one day Nemo invited him to go ashore to see something of great importance. Aronnax felt that at last he was to have his answer.

The two men got into the skiff—
a small boat that was kept on top
of the submarine. Sailors rowed
them to a mountainous island.

Nemo led Aronnax to the top of a
hill, and they seated themselves
behind a rock. The Captain pointed
down to the shore on the far side

of the island. Gangs of ragged prisoners were carrying heavy bags to a ship tied up at a wharf.

"What is this place?" Aronnax asked.

"The prison camp of Rorapandi, run by the most hateful nation in the world. Prisoners of war are kept here. Take a good look. Here—use my telescope."

Through the telescope Aronnax saw men in chains stumbling under their heavy loads. Armed guards whipped them onward.

"Good heavens!" he gasped. "What is in those sacks they are carrying?"

"Nitrates for making gunpowder —the seeds of war! The prisoners are loading a cargo of death in that ship. And if the ship were to take it home, the world would die a little

more. I was once a slave in that camp, Professor. Look at it again. I don't want you to forget what you have seen here today."

Aronnax turned away. "I have seen enough."

While being rowed back in the skiff, Nemo told more of his own story. "I did not escape from that prison camp alone. There were others, and most of them are still with me."

"The crew of the *Nautilus*?"

"Yes. Like myself, they are men with a purpose."

"How did you escape, Captain?"

"We captured one of the enemy's ships. Then we fled to an island that is not on any chart but my own. A place known to me as Vulcania."

"Vulcania? It sounds far away."

"Far away and useful. It is a dead

volcano with a power station hidden in its hollow core. We built the *Nautilus* there. Before long, Professor, you will see Vulcania with your own eyes. When our business here is finished, the *Nautilus* is going home."

When they reached the submarine, the First Mate met them on the deck. "We arrived at this island just in time, Captain. The nitrate ship is getting ready to leave."

"Very good. That ship will sail with the tide at sunset, but her evil cargo will never reach its port. You have your orders."

"Aye, aye, sir." He called down the hatch, "All hands to attack stations!"

Nemo said sharply, "Go below, Professor."

Aronnax frowned. "You mean—you are going to *sink* that ship?"

Nemo's eyes flashed. "Go below, I said! And stay in your quarters!"

A half-hour before sunset, Captain Nemo sat down at his pipe organ and began to play wild music. His grim face was beaded with sweat. Booming chords echoed throughout the submarine. Ned and Conseil closed the door of their cabin, trying to block out the sound. In his own quarters, Aronnax stopped writing in his journal and covered his ears with his hands.

Just as the music rose to a crashing peak, an alarm bell sounded. Nemo left the organ and climbed the stairs to the wheelhouse of the *Nautilus*. Through the window he saw the nitrate ship a mile dead ahead. She was nosing her way beyond the shelter of the island.

Nemo gripped the wheel and shouted commands. "We stay on the surface—on a crash course! Full speed ahead!"

With her two big headlights glowing like monster's eyes, the *Nautilus* sped toward the doomed ship. The submarine struck her just below the waterline, cutting her in two. Coming out into open water on the other side, the *Nautilus* turned quickly so that Nemo could watch the result. Within seconds the nitrate ship exploded with a terrifying flash.

In their quarters Aronnax, Conseil, and Ned had been thrown against the walls by the crash. They ran to the viewport in the salon just in time to see the explosion.

"Heaven help them!" cried Aronnax.

Conseil moaned. "All those men —they didn't even have a chance."

Ned Land pounded the wall with his fist. "They were all sailors, same as me, Professor! All murdered by that pirate you're tryin' to make friends with!"

They were staring out at the remains of the nitrate ship when Nemo came up behind them.

"Back to your quarters!" he commanded. "All of you!"

Ned and Conseil obeyed sullenly, but Aronnax stayed and faced Nemo. Before he could speak, the First Mate appeared.

"Damage report, Captain. Rudder is broken."

Nemo nodded. "We'll make repairs here."

"Aye, aye, sir."

Nemo turned to Aronnax. "I asked you to leave, Professor."

Aronnax glared at him. "You also asked me to look at that prison camp. To show me how badly those guards treated their war prisoners. Why? To make me think you did right by sinking their ship? You are a murderer, Captain!"

Nemo's eyes flashed. "Those few men were dealers in death! I have paid them back for the thousands whom they have helped kill in wars. And for what they did to me. They have taken everything from me, Professor—everything but my secret. The secret of the *Nautilus* and the power that drives her. They threw me into prison, and when they failed to learn my secret"—his voice

fell to a hoarse whisper—"they killed my wife and son." He seated himself wearily and looked up. "Do you understand the meaning of hate, Professor?"

"I am sure I do."

"Perhaps. But what you do not understand is the *power* of hate. Hate can fill the heart as surely as love can."

Messages in Bottles

When Aronnax returned to his quarters he found Conseil on the floor reading his journal.

"Give me that!" he said angrily. "What do you mean by reading my journal?"

Conseil turned red. "I—I wasn't really reading it, Professor. When we rammed that ship, things were thrown all over. I was just trying to tidy up in here." The little student got to his feet. "Professor, I'd like to speak to you."

"What about?"

"If you'll excuse me for saying so, I think things have gone far enough. Murder means nothing to Nemo. I think he really enjoys it." '

"It is not your place to judge," Aronnax said sternly. "With the power at his command, Nemo could do great good in the world. I must make him understand that. When the time comes he will judge himself. Now please go away and leave me alone."

Feeling hurt and a little angry, Conseil hurried to the cabin he shared with Ned. "I want to talk to you about the Professor," he said. "I think Nemo has won him over."

Ned shrugged. "What did you expect? The Professor's so interested in Nemo's fancy boat and great brain, he can't see anythin' else."

Conseil nodded unhappily. "All he ever talks about is the good that Nemo could do. He keeps making excuses for that madman. That's why it's important for you and me to be friends, Ned."

"Yeah? All I want is to escape."

"So do I—with you and the Professor. Nemo has won him over, but we've got to save him in spite of himself. You once said you have a plan. Is that true?"

"Sure I got a plan. Trouble is it won't work."

"Why not?"

" 'Cause I can't figure where we're headin'. If I could we'd have a chance."

Conseil lowered his voice. "I know where we're heading. I read it in the Professor's journal. Nemo told him we're going to his home base—a volcanic island called Vulcania. But it's not marked on any chart but his own."

Ned clapped him on the back, almost knocking him over. "Holy smoke! This is what I've been waitin' for! If I can just sneak into the chartroom and have a look at that chart. Come on—I'll need you to keep watch for me."

Quietly they crept along the hallway toward the chartroom. Before they got to it, Nemo, the First Mate, and two sailors came out, carrying wrenches and crowbars.

"We're in luck," Ned whispered.

"They're goin' outside to repair the rudder. Keep your eyes peeled while I go in there and look for that chart."

While Conseil stood watch outside, Ned unrolled chart after chart without finding the right one. Suddenly Conseil rushed in, looking frightened. "The Mate's coming! If they catch us here, Nemo will throw us overboard!"

Ned shoved him through a door at the other end of the chartroom and followed, closing the door behind them. Through a peephole he saw the Mate looking around suspiciously. Ned braced himself for a fight. But the Mate turned and went out.

"Wow, that was close!" Ned said.

Conseil felt something brush against his leg. He gave a shriek.

Ned laughed. "Take it easy. It's only Esmeralda."

"Oh, yes—the seal. But she scared me half to death." He glanced around, his big eyes bulging. "Say, this is Nemo's private cabin! Let's get out of here!"

"Wait!" Ned's eye had been caught by a chart on the wall.

"What is it?"

"This chart. I bet it's the one we've been lookin' for."

Esmeralda wanted to play. She barked and gave Ned a sharp poke in the chest.

"Hey! Cut it out," Ned said. "Conseil, fetch me that pencil and paper from Nemo's desk. Quick!"

Grabbing for the pencil, Conseil upset Nemo's cigar container. Cigars fell all over the desk. Barking happily, Esmeralda swallowed one as if it were a fish.

"She loves 'em," Ned said. "While I get to work here, keep feedin' her cigars. That'll keep her quiet."

The seal barked again and got another cigar. Ned put his finger on a dot in the very center of the chart. "Look! All the distances here are measured out from this point. It's the center of everything. It's got to be Vulcania!"

"Can't you please hurry?" Conseil whined. "They'll be coming back any minute."

"Eat a cigar yourself and shut up!

I'm busy." Studying the chart, Ned scribbled on the paper while Conseil fed the hungry seal. "Got it!" Ned said finally. "Let's go."

"Too late," Conseil wailed. "I hear them coming back."

"Too late, my foot! Out this other door!" He threw the seal a cigar and followed Conseil through the door. A second later Captain Nemo entered his cabin from the chartroom.

"Why, Esmeralda," they heard Nemo say. "You've eaten a whole week's supply of my cigars! I rather hope you get a stomach ache."

"We barely escaped with our skins!" Conseil said when they were back in their own cabin. "What were you copying in there?"

"The location of Vulcania, what do ya think? Get me six of those bottles from the closet—the kind Nemo collects fish and stuff in."

Conseil brought them. "Here. What are you going to do with them?"

"Put messages in 'em and throw 'em overboard."

"Oh, come now! Messages in bottles went out a hundred and fifty years ago with Robinson Crusoe."

"Maybe so, but they still might work." Ned tore a sheet of paper into six small pieces and began to write on them. "Now suppose you give your tongue a vacation while I tell the rest of the world where they can find us."

When Ned was finished, each of the six bottles contained the message: ARONNAX AND PARTY ARE CAPTIVES ABOARD MONSTER SUBMARINE BOAT BASED 12 DEGREES 19 MINUTES SOUTH LATITUDE, 169 DEGREES 28 MINUTES WEST LONGITUDE.

That night, when the *Nautilus* was cruising on the surface, Ned threw the six bottles overboard. They went floating off into the darkness.

The Giant Squid

One morning a month later, when the *Nautilus* was running through a group of islands, her rudder broke down again. Nemo tried to keep the ship on a straight course but failed. She crashed onto a coral reef and jolted to a stop. Aronnax and his two companions hurried to the wheelhouse. Nemo was there talking with his engineer.

"An accident, Captain?" asked the Professor.

"A slight one. Our broken rudder has put us on a reef. The tide will float us free by evening. We're just off the coast of New Guinea, Professor. Would you like to go ashore?"

"No, thank you. The last time we went ashore it led to murder."

Ned scowled. "Hey, Professor, how can you throw away a chance like that? Fresh air, dry land, coconuts, mangoes?" He turned to Nemo. "I'd like to go ashore in his place, Captain. What do you say?"

"Very well, Mr. Land, you may go. But I must warn you not to try to escape into the jungle."

Ned put on a hurt look. "Me escape? Never! How can you even think such a thing?"

"Easily. For your own good, stay on the beach. The natives are cannibals. They eat liars as well as honest men."

Hurrying up to the deck, Ned unbolted the skiff. He rowed toward the island, happy as a clam. Dancing in his head were visions of food, freedom, and pretty girls. When the skiff nosed onto the sandy beach, he leaped ashore and waved good-bye to the submarine. Singing "Got a Whale of a Tale to Tell Ya, Lads," he went racing into the jungle.

Ten minutes later he came running back to the beach, chased by screaming natives with long, sharp spears. He jumped into the skiff and rowed like a demon. Spears splashed all around him.

"Cannibals!" he shouted. "Help!

Hey, everybody—cannibals!''

Nemo and his repair crew were working outside when Ned pulled the skiff onto the deck. ''Cannibals!'' he yelled. ''Ya know what, Captain? They were gonna kill me!''

Nemo looked up calmly. ''Why shouldn't they kill you, Mr. Land? They didn't like your stepping onto their private island. So they decided to punish you in their own way.''

''Yeah, but—''

''Silence!'' Nemo thundered.

''You went into the jungle hoping to escape. And now you're going to regret it.'' He waved his hand. ''Take him below and lock him up.''

''Aye, aye, sir.''

''As soon as these repairs are made, Mr. Land, I'll see that you trouble me no longer.''

Yelling and struggling, Ned was dragged into the submarine and locked up in a small cabin.

By mid-afternoon the rudder was working again, and by early evening the tide floated the *Nautilus* off the

reef. Nemo and the Mate went forward to the wheelhouse to start the submarine.

Before the first order was given, an excited message came through the speaking-tube. "Emergency! Giant squid astern!"

Nemo looked out at the back of the ship. "Emergency speed! All engines!"

But the squid reached the submarine before she could escape. Then began the most desperate battle in the history of the *Nautilus*.

It was a fight for life. The squid had ten arms and was twice the size of the submarine. Wrapping its tentacles around the boat, the monster tried to crush the *Nautilus*.

"We must kill it quickly!" Nemo cried. "All hands to the base of the chartroom hatch!"

The crew gathered at the ladder, armed with axes and harpoons. Nemo said grimly, "Men, you'll be fighting with the most dangerous beast in the sea. Stay clear of its tentacles. They'll grab anything

within reach and hang on to it forever! When you strike a blow, remember—the only vital spot is squarely between the eyes! You must hit the squid there to kill it!"

He threw a switch, opening the hatch. At once a great, slimy tentacle reached down into the room.

"Stand back!" Nemo cried.

The horrid arm was dotted with suction cups. It lashed from side to side, seeking a living thing to crush and kill.

Nemo ordered his men to follow him to the forward hatch. He climbed out on deck, harpoon in hand. "Stand clear!" he screamed as the men joined him. At once they were faced with two more of the ugly, whipping tentacles. Dodging under one of them, Nemo aimed his harpoon and threw it. He hit the beast above one of its eyes but not in the vital spot between them.

The angered squid opened and closed its big parrotlike beak. "Throw me another harpoon!" Nemo shouted. As he turned to catch the weapon, he was caught by a tentacle and pinned to the deck.

The Mate rushed to free him with his ax, but couldn't get close enough.

Alarmed by the noise above, Aronnax and Conseil hurried toward the chartroom hatch. They saw the squid's tentacle still reaching blindly for its prey.

"Good heavens!" Aronnax cried. "Ned! Ned, where are you?"

"In here," came a voice. "In this room behind you. Unlock the door!"

Conseil turned the key and Ned burst from his prison.

"Careful!" Aronnax warned. "The tentacle!"

Ned's eyes lit up. "A giant squid! I'll be a mermaid's uncle!"

A sailor came down from the other hatch and spied Ned. "Mr. Land! Come up and help us! The

Captain's in danger!"

Ned bounded up to the deck. He was just in time to see Nemo dragged into the water by the tentacle. Snatching a harpoon from one of the sailors, he took aim and let fly. The weapon passed between the deadly arms of the squid and buried itself in the head, right between the eyes. Almost at once the beast began to sink. It pulled Nemo down with it.

Whipping out his sheath-knife, Ned dived beneath the surface and cut Nemo free. In a moment he appeared again, holding Nemo's head above the water. He grabbed a line thrown by the Mate, and he and Nemo were pulled up to the deck.

Aronnax and Conseil were at the foot of the ladder when Nemo came down, helped by the Mate. As Ned appeared, breathless and dripping, Nemo looked up and spoke in a weak voice.

"Mr. Land, you—you saved my life. Why?"

"A good question, Captain." Ned shrugged. "Darned if I know the answer."

The next morning when Ned woke up, he was surprised to find Esmeralda sitting beside his bunk. She barked happily and kissed him on the nose. He laughed. "Hey, Esmie, your whiskers tickle. You oughta shave, baby. You're beginnin' to look like Nemo."

Conseil came in with some coffee. "I'm glad you're not locked up any more, Ned. I was afraid the Captain was going to do something awful to you."

"Yeah, I've got the run of the boat." Ned grunted. "Big-hearted Nemo."

"The Professor's happy, too. You know, it's the first time he's seen Nemo show any human feelings."

"I don't care what he shows—and neither does Esmeralda, do ya, honey?" The seal barked and gave him a wet kiss. "I'm gettin' off this iron pot some day, Esmie. And when I do, you're goin' along with me. That's a promise, baby."

Farewell to the *Nautilus*

Some days later the *Nautilus* surfaced and moved toward an island in the distance. In the Captain's cabin, Nemo and Aronnax were having a serious talk.

"No doubt," said Nemo, "you think your Mr. Land is a hero for saving my life, do you not?"

"He did what he thought was right, Captain. And I know you

were deeply touched by his brave act. But you are ashamed to admit it."

"Oh, really? Why do you say that?"

"Because your life is built on hate. You are afraid to admit that you have any kinder feelings, and that the rest of mankind has them, too. You are afraid of discovering that your way of life is a mistake."

Nemo curled his lip. "And you are too soft-hearted, my dear Professor. My life beneath the sea is perfect. Life in the world above is not."

Aronnax leaned forward. "But you can change all that, don't you see? You could lead mankind down the right path—if only you would share your scientific knowledge."

"Ha! You really believe men would lay down their arms, stop killing each other, and do away with their slave camps?"

"I think *I* could talk them into it. Let me try."

Nemo pointed to his chart. "We are nearing Vulcania. In a few hours we will arrive. There, inside the hollow mountain, you will see my power station and other secrets. Secrets for which my enemies have hunted me!" He pounded the chart with his fist. "But the power is still mine! Enough energy to save the world—or destroy it!"

The First Mate entered. "Emergency, Captain! Warships dead ahead—between us and Vulcania!"

Nemo turned to Aronnax, his face red with anger. "You asked if I would share my knowledge. There's your answer! My home is being attacked by the same men that you wish to make friends with!"

Aronnax followed Nemo and the Mate into the wheelhouse. Nemo peered ahead through his telescope. Groups of armed men were moving like ants up the sides of the volcano.

"Their landing parties have already reached my island," Nemo said grimly. "This is a dark hour for mankind, Professor." He barked orders to the Mate. "They'll be at the top in twenty minutes! When they come down inside, our power station must be destroyed! Prepare to dive! Four degrees down and ahead full!"

"Aye, aye, sir."

With Captain Nemo at the wheel, the *Nautilus* dived and went ahead through an underwater tunnel. It led to a lagoon in the hollow core of the volcano. The boat surfaced in the lagoon and cut across to a huge power station on the opposite shore.

"Stop all engines!" Nemo commanded. "Break out the skiff!"

Followed by the Mate, he raced

down the ladder from the wheel-house. The Professor came down more slowly and found Ned and Conseil at the bottom.

"Hey, what's all the excitement?" Ned asked.

"We are at Nemo's base," said Aronnax, "and the island is surrounded by warships."

"Warships?" Ned's eyes widened. "Hey, I bet they found my bottles with the notes in 'em! Come on—let's go topside and see what we can do to escape!"

From the open hatch, they saw Nemo being rowed in the skiff toward a pier. When he reached it, he leaped out and raced into the power station.

Conseil pointed upward. "Look!"

Soldiers were moving down from the rim of the volcano, firing at the *Nautilus* as they came. Aronnax and Conseil ducked down inside the hatch. But Ned jumped up on deck and tore off his shirt. "I'm gonna let 'em know we're here!" he shouted.

"No, Ned, don't!" Aronnax cried.

Ned waved his shirt, yelling like a demon as bullets sprayed the deck

around him. "Hey, you men up there—we're friends! Don't shoot! We're friends, I tell ya! We're the ones that threw the bottles overboard!" But the firing didn't stop. With a curse, Ned gave up and took cover below.

Moments later the skiff returned to its place on the deck. The oarsmen ran to the hatch. Nemo hurried behind them in a rain of bullets. As he started down the ladder, he suddenly stiffened and gave a cry. Then he continued slowly down into the submarine. Blood spread across the back of his jacket.

In the wheelhouse Nemo gave orders to dive. Biting his lip in pain, he guided the *Nautilus* back through the tunnel into the open sea.

"Slow engines," he said in a voice that could barely be heard. "All controls eight degrees down."

As the *Nautilus* headed toward the bottom, he tied the wheel in place and staggered back to the salon. Aronnax, Ned, Conseil, and the crew were waiting for him there. The crewmen's faces were lined with grief.

Held up by the Mate, Nemo said, "Men, we are taking the *Nautilus* down for the last time."

The crewmen nodded. "We understand, sir," said the Mate, "and we're with you—to the end."

Ned shouted at Nemo, "Hey, wait a minute, I don't understand! What's that got to do with *us?*"

"I am dying, Mr. Land. And the *Nautilus* and everyone aboard are dying with me." He turned to Aronnax. "Professor, in a short time an explosion will destroy my island and all its works. That is why I have brought the *Nautilus* deep under the sea, to her last resting place. Here we will die in peace. Now let every man go to his quarters and remain there."

All the crewmen but the Mate went out quietly. "I'll stay here with you, Captain," said the Mate.

Conseil let out a moan. "No—I don't want to die!"

"Me neither," said Ned, darting forward.

Aronnax grabbed Ned's arm and spoke to Nemo. "Captain, you cannot do this. There is more at stake here than just our lives. You made a dream of the future come true. At least let your ship live, so that it may show the world what you knew. I beg you to change your mind!"

Nemo answered slowly, his eyes half-closed with pain. "No, Professor. The world is not yet ready for a new and better life. But there is hope for the future. One day others will rediscover what I have learned. In God's good time."

Aronnax turned to Ned and Conseil. "I am sorry, my dear friends. It seems there is nothing we can do."

"Bunk!" Ned cried. "We're not gonna lie down and die like the rest of 'em! Come on—we're takin' over this iron pot!" He started toward the wheelhouse and received a hard blow on the jaw from the Mate. Swinging with his right, then his left, Ned gave the Mate two smashes in return. Trading punches that rocked them both, they fought until Ned got in the winning blow. He left the Mate out cold on the floor.

"Wait here!" Ned shouted to Aronnax and Conseil. "I'm gonna bring this tub to the surface!" In the wheelhouse he shoved up levers and turned the control arm. With terrible slowness the *Nautilus* rose to the surface. Then the ship started forward but grounded on a coral reef.

Rushing back to the salon, Ned found his friends waiting. "Where's Nemo?" he asked.

"We carried him back to his

cabin," said the Professor. "He cannot last much longer."

Ned hurried his friends toward the hatch. "Come on—we're on the surface. Let's get out of here fast!"

On deck they pushed the skiff into the water and climbed in. "Everybody grab oars and start pullin' hard!" Ned yelled. "That whole island's gonna blow up any second!"

Esmeralda barked at them from the deck. "Come on, Esmie baby!" Ned called. "I promised you'd come along, so jump in!"

Esmeralda leaped into the skiff and lay down between the rowers.

"All set now—pull!" When the men had gone a fair distance from the grounded submarine, a dull boom came across the sea. The sound grew to a roar as they rowed, their eyes fixed on the island. Then suddenly Vulcania exploded in a

flash of orange. Clouds of fire and steam shot upward, widening at the top and coloring the sea and sky.

Ned gave a whoop. "Thar she blows!"

In the midst of the explosion, the *Nautilus* slipped from the reef and began to sink, stern first, carrying the crew down with her. As she tilted upward, a deep cut showed in her bottom plates.

Aronnax rested on his oars, shaking his head. "A pity," he murmured. "If Captain Nemo had loved instead of hated, he might have led the world to everlasting peace."

The *Nautilus* had carried the three men 20,000 leagues under the sea, more than twice the distance around the earth. But as they watched in awed silence, the great submarine went down for the last time.

Man-Eaters!

IMAGINE a hot summer day. You and your family have gone to the beach. You are playing in the water near the shore. Other people are swimming nearby. Suddenly someone yells, "Shark!" You dash out of the water as fast as you can. So does everyone else. Your parents pack up their belongings and take you right home. Within fifteen minutes, everyone is gone from the beach. No one wants to be near a shark.

Why is everyone so afraid? Because sharks have attacked, hurt, and even killed many people. That is why they are often called "man-eaters." But strangely, only about 25 of the 250 kinds of sharks that exist ever bother people. The rest leave us alone. Unfortunately, they all get the blame for the danger caused by a few.

Those few sharks, however, can be *pretty* dangerous. For example, at times the great white shark will attack anything in the water that moves. A single vicious bite by this man-eater can cut a full-grown person in half.

"Man-eating" sharks usually eat fish or shellfish. But from time to time they attack fishing boats or swimmers. Yet often, they will swim past a deep-sea diver and pay no attention to him. No one is sure why sharks behave in such a strange way. But scientists do know a few facts about them.

Every shark depends mainly on its nose to find food. The hungrier a shark is, the more sensitive its nose is to smell. The slightest trace of blood in the water will attract a shark at once. Even when scientists have blindfolded a shark, it can follow the trail of a wounded fish. So if you have an open wound, you should not go swimming in the ocean.

Before closing in for the kill, sharks usually circle their victims. One kind of shark, the thresher shark, sweeps its long, curved tail about to herd a school of fish into a position where the fish can be killed and eaten. Sometimes a team of threshers work together to keep fish trapped in a bay. Then other threshers can strike them with their tails and eat them.

Very often a group of sharks become so excited while feeding that they bite at anything and every-thing. The more they snap—often at each other—the more excited they become. Scientists say the sharks are in a "feeding frenzy."

While sharks are in a feeding frenzy, they gobble down practically anything in their way. In the stomachs of captured sharks, scientists have found such objects as rubber tires, tin cans, wood beams, logs, and parts of boats.

People know a shark is near when they see one of its back fins sticking out of the water. That's when somebody yells, "Shark!" and all the swimmers dash out of the water.

Look! A hammerhead shark!

And they should. The fin's appearance means the shark is swimming near the surface. It does this when it is excited, hungry, and cruising for food.

Besides this famous back fin, shaped like a triangle, a shark has one other fin on its back. It also has two sets of fins along the sides of its body. The pair nearest the head stands out stiffly. This helps a shark keep its balance as it streaks through the water. Because sharks have large fins, strong tails, and great muscular power, many of them can move at super speeds.

Muscle power makes a shark's jaws incredibly strong, too. Inside those powerful jaws are razor-sharp teeth that grow larger as the animal gets older. But one kind of shark—the whale shark—has tiny teeth that cannot hurt anyone. Strangely, this shark is the largest shark of all.

Behind the first row of a shark's teeth are other rows of teeth. As a shark's outer row wears out, it uses the next row to bite and chew. It uses up several rows of teeth during its lifetime.

A shark's skin is almost as sharp as its teeth. Most fish are slimy to touch. But the shark feels as rough as sandpaper. In fact, some woodworkers use sharkskin instead of regular sandpaper on their wood.

Although sharks have been living in the seas for millions of years, scientists still do not know a great deal about them. One way scientists hope to learn more is by tagging. A tag is shot from a gun into a shark's back fin. This does not harm the shark. The tag has information in many languages about the shark's habits. Later, if the shark is caught off the shore of another country, information about it can be sent back to the original taggers. In this way, scientists can gather and study the whole life history of a shark.

Watch out for a shark's strong jaws and sharp teeth.

Diving for Treasure

Dɪᴅ ʏᴏᴜ ᴇᴠᴇʀ ᴅʀᴇᴀᴍ of sunken treasure—piles and piles of gold and silver coins lying at the bottom of the ocean? Well, sunken treasure doesn't just appear in dreams and storybooks. Many ships carrying valuable loads really are lying on the bottom of the sea.

The ship *Chameau* (sham-ᴏʜ) was loaded with gold and silver when it sank near the coast of Canada. Over two hundred years later, a young diver accidentally spotted the wreck—and found real sunken treasure. But not everyone who searched for the *Chameau* was as lucky—or as patient—as he was.

The Wreck

The warship *Chameau* sailed from France in the summer of 1725. She was headed for Canada, carrying 300 passengers and a load of gold and silver. The money would be one year's pay for the French soldiers at Louisbourg, a fort on the east coast of Canada.

The voyage took two months. At last the *Chameau* neared Louisbourg. But late one night a storm hit. The rough sea tossed the *Chameau* about. The captain tried to head for the Louisbourg harbor, but the ship struck jagged rocks. With a terrible crash, the wooden ship split open. Icy water rushed in. Just a few minutes later, the whole ship disappeared into the sea. Not one passenger survived. The ship and the treasure lay scattered on the ocean floor.

A Chilly Search

The French army had a simple plan to get their treasure back. A boat would tow a rope along behind it. At the end of the rope, a big hook—something like an anchor—would drag along the ocean floor. Perhaps the hook would catch on some part of the *Chameau* wreckage. Then men would dive at that spot to look for the treasure.

But the army's plan did not work. The hook caught on to many things, but never the *Chameau*. Time after time the men dived. But they found only rocks and old anchors and cannon. The cannon might have belonged to the *Chameau*. But the men did not see the treasure anywhere nearby. And they did not stay in the water very long searching, for it was icy cold. The sea off

Louisbourg never gets warmer than 45 degrees Fahrenheit (7 degrees Celsius). In contrast, most swimming pools today are heated to about 80 degrees F. (27 degrees C.). In the 1700s divers did not have protective rubber suits like the ones divers wear today. Instead they covered their bodies with a layer of grease. But the grease did not keep them very warm in the cold ocean. No wonder they gave up looking for the treasure after just one month.

Unlucky Treasure-Hunters

For many years afterwards, the people of Louisbourg talked and dreamed of the *Chameau*'s treasure. Every now and then, groups of

divers explored the area. They did not find the wreck. One group used a stick that they thought would point to anything made of gold. All they found was an old cannon. Some fishermen in the area said they had caught a bag of coins in their fish-net. But they said the bag broke and the money fell back into the ocean.

In 1914, a diver was searching a ship that had recently sunk near Louisbourg. While he was diving, he saw something glittering on the ocean floor. He looked more closely and saw gold and silver coins! He knew they must have come from the famous *Chameau*. He returned to his boat and decided to go back for the treasure after he had finished work on the newer wreck. He remembered the spot where he had seen the coins. But he didn't have a chance to go back. Just a few days later, he drowned while diving. He didn't even have a chance to tell anyone else where the treasure was.

A Lucky Dive and Some Hard Work

About 50 years later, a young diver named Alex Storm was luckier. He was also searching a recent wreck when he saw something that made his heart beat faster. He did not see coins—but he saw some

cannon. He knew the *Chameau* had gone down near that very spot. The cannon must have belonged to her. He dived again. This time he found a silver coin! Storm dived many more times, but that one coin was the only treasure he found. He knew there had to be more. If he could find the main body of the wrecked *Chameau,* perhaps he would find the rest of the treasure.

During the summer of 1961, Storm spent his spare time looking for the *Chameau*. But he could not find the treasure. In 1965, he finally decided to spend all his time on the search. He and two partners bought a boat. They studied old charts and ocean currents. They tried to figure out where the wrecked ship might have drifted.

For weeks the men dived in the icy-cold water. Winds made the ocean surface choppy. Underwater currents made diving difficult. The divers wore air tanks on their backs. They could usually stay underwater

for only an hour or so before their air would run out. Sometimes they had to return to the boat because they couldn't stand the cold water anymore.

They had company underwater, too. Playful seals followed the divers and watched curiously. Other visitors were not so welcome. Mackerel sharks, blue sharks, and basking sharks were also attracted by the divers' activities. Basking sharks can be up to 40 feet (about 12 meters) long—about as long as a bus. Work is very hard when a creature that big is looking over your shoulder!

So the search was not easy. Also, it was taking too long. The end of the summer was near, and the weather would soon make diving impossible. To speed up the search, Storm

and his partners decided to let the boat do some of the work. They made a sled and tied it to the boat with a rope. Now the divers could ride underwater while the boat towed them along. They rode just above the rocky ocean bottom, looking for clues that would lead them to the treasure.

At last one day in late September, the divers' patience and hard work paid off. They found the hold, or storage space, of the *Chameau*. And inside were stacks and stacks of silver and gold coins! The silver coins were now a dull gray, but there was no doubt: This was real sunken treasure! The divers loaded the coins into canvas bags. Then they used a basket on a rope to raise the bags onto the ship.

The three partners continued to dive. They brought up thousands of coins, a watch, glass, pottery, silverware, and metal fittings from the ship. By the time they were through, they had found at least 750,000 dollars' worth of treasure! The Canadian government claimed one-tenth of it. The three divers shared the rest. They sold most of the coins to coin collectors. You can see some of the other things the divers found on the *Chameau* at a small museum in Louisbourg, Nova Scotia.

This proof of treasure on the ocean bottom may make you eager to try treasure-hunting yourself. There are still so many treasure ships on the ocean floor that some divers can make their living searching shipwrecks. But remember, diving for treasure is hard and dangerous work. As the *Chameau* divers found out, it takes a lot of knowledge and patience—and a little luck!

Ocean Scientist

THE OCEAN IS a mysterious and exciting place. Scientists use complicated and expensive equipment to study it. But you can do many simple water experiments right at home. And they won't cost you a million dollars! For example, you can make your own icebergs, and you can make a submarine that goes up and down in water.

Let's start with the submarine. Here's what you'll need:

A tall, clear glass bottle. (A quart or liter pop bottle works well.)
A glass eyedropper. (A plastic one won't work. Buy a glass eyedropper at any drugstore for about a quarter.)
Plastic wrap or a piece of balloon
A rubber band
Water

Fill the bottle to the top with water. Dip the eyedropper in the water and squeeze the bulb. Keep drawing water until the eyedropper is about half full. Then place it inside the bottle, in the water. The eyedropper is your "submarine." It should float deep in the bottle. Only the top of the bulb should stick out above the water's surface. You may need to experiment with the amount of water in the eyedropper to make it float properly.

Now stretch the plastic wrap (or balloon) over the bottle top. Fasten the wrap tightly with a rubber band so it is taut like the head of a drum.

Push down on the plastic with your thumb. The submarine will dive down to the bottom of the bottle. When you let up the pressure of your thumb, the sub will return to the surface. (The first time you press down, your thumb may hit the dropper's bulb. But afterwards, the dropper will stay deep enough in the water so you won't touch it.) You can move your sub up and down as you like. Simply put more or less pressure on the bottle top. How does this work?

Watch the eyedropper carefully as it sinks. Do you see that a small amount of water is going into it? When you press down on the plastic, you are putting pressure on the air at the top of the bottle. The air is squashed down, or compressed. The compressed air puts pressure on the water. But water can't be compressed the way air can. Instead, the water spreads. It goes into the only space around—the eyedropper—compressing the air inside. The weight of the extra water in the eyedropper makes the dropper heavier—and it sinks. As you let up the pressure on the bottle top, some of the water comes back out of the eyedropper. Your submarine then becomes lighter. It rises toward the surface again.

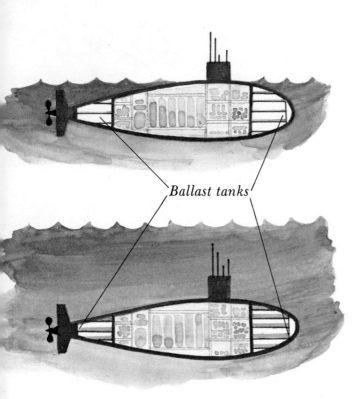

Ballast tanks

If you took off a submarine's outer covering, this is what you would see.

Real submarines sink and rise in much the same way. The subs are built with large tanks, called ballast tanks. To make a sub dive, the ballast tanks are opened and filled with ocean water. The more water let into the tanks, the lower the sub will go. To make the submarine rise, compressed air forces the water out of the ballast tanks.

Are you ready for the iceberg experiment? You can start this one today, but you'll have to wait until tomorrow to finish it.

What is an iceberg? It's a giant chunk of ice and compressed snow. Icebergs float in the waters near the North and South poles. In 1912 a ship called the *Titanic* sank when it hit an iceberg in the North Atlantic Ocean. Since then an ice patrol searches for icebergs. It reports their positions so that this kind of accident won't happen again. When you make your own iceberg, you will see how easy it would be for a ship to run into the underwater part of an iceberg.

Another danger of icebergs is that they roll over as they melt. The flip-flop causes enormous waves that sometimes damage nearby boats. Your iceberg won't make a giant wave, but it probably will turn over as it melts.

What you'll need:

*A plastic sandwich bag and
    twist tie*
Food coloring
*A clear glass bowl. (A deep
    Pyrex casserole or a fruit
    bowl is fine.)*
The use of a freezer
Water

Start your iceberg the night before you plan to do the experiment. Fill one corner of the plastic bag with water. Add two or three drops of food coloring to the water. A little above the water line, twist the bag closed. Tie it tightly with the twist tie. Then set it on the freezer shelf. This will give you a short, fat iceberg. If you have wire shelves in your freezer, you can make a taller iceberg. Tie the bag to one of the wires, and let the bag hang down. Keep the bag in the freezer overnight.

For the experiment itself, fill the bowl about two-thirds full of warm water. Place the bowl in front of a window so that you get a clear view through the side of the bowl. Take your iceberg from the freezer. Peel off the plastic bag, and put the iceberg into the water.

Do you see how much of the iceberg is under the water? Icebergs usually float with only one-eighth showing above the water. You can see how dangerous this could be to an unsuspecting ship.

Now watch through the side of the bowl as the iceberg melts. See how the colored cold water drops down and settles on the bottom of the bowl. It happens because cold water is denser than warm water. This means that the tiny bits, or particles, that make up cold water are closer together than the particles that make up warm water. The cold water sinks to the bottom and pushes the warm water to the top.

You may even be able to feel the glass at the bottom of the bowl getting colder.

Is your iceberg twisting and turning? Has it flipped over? As parts of the iceberg melt away, the place where most of the iceberg's weight is centered changes. So if a large chunk melts or breaks off the bottom, the bottom becomes lighter than the top. And the iceberg flips over.

Now that you have done two ocean experiments, would you like to do more? Would you like to be an ocean scientist? You certainly have a good head start!

A famous photo taken at Loch Ness. Is this really Nessie?

Nessie, Nessie, Come Out If You Are

WHAT CREATURE IS about 45 feet long and has a funny name? Why Nessie, of course! Nessie, better known as the Loch Ness Monster, lives in a Scottish lake called Loch Ness. For close to 1,500 years, people have claimed that they have seen a monster in that lake. They have told of a gigantic head, back, tail, or other parts. At least 4,000 people have seen some form of unknown monster in Loch Ness. Some people have even reported a monster on land near the lake. Books have been written about Nessie. And photographs have been taken of some sort of large creature in Loch Ness.

What Is Loch Ness Like?

The Scottish lake is about 25 miles (40 kilometers) long and very deep. In one place it is about 970 feet (291 meters) deep. The water is filled with bits of moss and other plants, so it is difficult for anyone to see very far down. But Loch Ness is certainly deep enough and large enough to be the home of a sea monster—or of many such creatures.

Loch Ness is warm enough for sea monsters, too. The water in Loch Ness is quite chilly, but it seldom freezes. The temperature in the winter hardly ever goes below 35 degrees Fahrenheit (about 1 degree Celsius).

Since 1847, Loch Ness and two other lakes have been part of a canal called the Caledonian Canal. A ship can travel across Scotland by way of this canal. It connects the North Sea and the Atlantic Ocean.

Then why hasn't Nessie left Loch Ness and traveled to the North Sea or the Atlantic Ocean? Because no 45-foot monster could swim through the canal—without getting caught. And being caught is something Nessie is very careful to avoid. The canal is made up of a series of gates. Between them the water is often shallow. The gates open and let some water in or out each time a ship has to pass through. Then the gates close again. If monsters do exist in Loch Ness, the gates block their exit through the canal.

The River Ness also connects Loch Ness to the sea. But it is a very shallow river. In fact, in many spots,

hardly any water runs through it at all. So no large monster could swim through this passageway either. It seems that Nessie must stay at home in the lake.

When Did Someone First See Nessie?

Sightings of unknown creatures have been reported since the year 565. The first report described a swimmer attacked by a monster in Loch Ness. However, it wasn't until 1933 that people really became interested in Nessie. In that year a new road was built along one side of the lake. Travel along the lake became easy. And from then on sighting of "something big in the water" became common. That's when people began to take seriously the idea of sea monsters in Loch Ness.

Some scientists and many other people honestly believe Nessie exists. But none of them is sure exactly what the Loch Ness Monster might be.

What Is Nessie Supposed to Look Like?

Photographs have helped to describe Nessie. Unfortunately, all of them have been somewhat blurred. The first known photograph taken

SCOTLAND

INVERNESS

ABERDEEN

GLASGOW

Loch Ness

Loch Ness

CALEDONIAN CANAL

River Ness

Loch Lachy

Loch Oich

CALEDONIAN CANAL

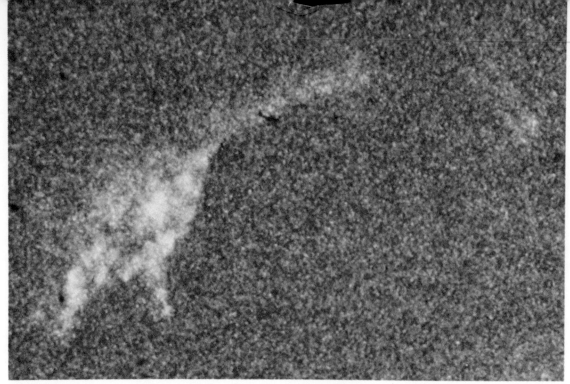

An underwater photograph of the Loch Ness Monster

at Loch Ness was in 1933. It showed something very large in the lake. But what that something was, was not clear. A few years later, another Loch Ness photograph became famous. It showed what appears to be a snakelike neck sticking out of the water.

Underwater photographs taken in 1975 by a group of scientists from Boston caused a lot of excitement. Those photographs show what might be the flippers, the body, and the head of an ugly monster swimming in Loch Ness waters.

From the photos and many sightings, a general description of Nessie would go something like this:

Color—black, gray, or rust.

Neck—snakelike and from 2 to 9 feet (60 to 270 centimeters) long.

Face—somewhat like either a snake or a dog.

Body—about 45 feet (13 meters), heavy, with a long tail and four diamond-shaped flippers.

Legs—none.

Personality—shy.

What Might Nessie Be?

Nessie might be an ancient reptile called a plesiosaur. At least many people think so. Although plesiosaurs supposedly died out about 70 million years ago, some could have survived in a lake as deep as Loch Ness. There, the reptiles would have been cut off from the rest of the world. They could have gone on having their

A plesiosaur. Could Nessie be one?

babies, keeping their kind alive long after others like them died out.

Some people believe Nessie is not a plesiosaur at all, but an escaped pet crocodile. Others think the monster may be a giant-sized newt (a kind of salamander), a large eel, a sea otter, a giant sea slug, a giant sea worm, a giant squid, or even a whale.

A recent theory is that Nessie may be a large seal. Seals have short necks, but the monster may be a kind of long-necked seal that scientists have never seen before.

Why Isn't Nessie Seen All the Time?

Some scientists think the shy monster spends much of its time in underwater caverns in the lake. These would be big enough to house families of very large creatures.

Nessie, Nessie, Come Out If You Are

The search for the Loch Ness Monster will continue until someone actually captures one. In the meantime, there's something exciting about searching for the unknown. Perhaps someday someone will prove to the world that there really is a monster living in Loch Ness. And perhaps that person will find Nessie by riding on the lake in a boat and saying the words,

"Nessie, Nessie, come out if you are!"

The Loch Ness Mystery

On Monday, Sleuth couldn't remember his name. On Tuesday, Sleuth forgot where he lived. And on Wednesday, Sleuth went out on a case without his trousers! Yes, there was no doubt about it. England's Greatest Detective was becoming absent-minded.

On Thursday, Mickey decided that something had to be done about Sleuth's memory. That's why, on Friday, Sleuth found himself in the office of Doctor Ivor Gett, England's Greatest Memory Expert.

"Sleuth's brain is overworked,"

Doctor Gett said to Mickey. "He needs a vacation. Take him someplace nice and quiet. And don't let him think for two weeks."

The next morning Mickey and Sleuth got on a train for Scotland. A few hours later they arrived at Loch Ness, the famous Scottish lake. By evening, they were settled comfortably in their rooms at the Loch Ness Hotel.

Early the next morning Mickey and Sleuth were awakened by a terrible commotion outside their door. They dressed quickly and went out into the hallway to see what was going on. All the hotel guests were running toward the front entrance.

"What's happening?" Mickey asked a man wearing a plaid kilt.

"It's the Loch Ness Monster!" he answered, without stopping. "It's in the lake!"

"Come on!" Mickey said to Sleuth. "And bring your camera."

Sleuth ran back into the room and grabbed his camera. Then the two friends ran down the hotel stairs and out the front door. The hotel guests were all down at the lake.

"There it is!" Sleuth exclaimed, pointing his camera at a big, green monster. It was cruising around in the middle of the lake. A few minutes later the monster sank below the waves and disappeared.

"So that was the famous Loch Ness Monster," Mickey said as they walked back to the hotel.

"What on earth!" Mickey exclaimed as he opened the door to the hotel room. The room was a mess. It looked as if a hurricane had hit it.

"We've been *robbed*!" Mickey said.

He and Sleuth checked their belongings quickly. "That's funny," Mickey said, scratching his head. "Nothing seems to be missing."

"Oh, but something *is* missing," Sleuth said. "My violin!"

Suddenly there was a knock on the door. It was the hotel manager.

"We've been robbed!" Mickey cried.

"Yes . . . I know," said the manager. "The whole hotel has been robbed. It happens every time the monster appears in the lake." He turned to Sleuth. "I need your help, Sleuth. You must solve this mystery."

"Sleuth can't solve any crimes for two weeks," Mickey said. "But I've learned a lot from working with Sleuth over the years. Perhaps I can help."

Meanwhile, far below the waters of the lake, the monster seems to be resting. But what's this? A porthole on the side of the Loch Ness Monster? And a light coming from inside? Why, it's not a monster at all. It's a cleverly disguised submarine! And look who's inside! Professor Nefarious and his evil henchmen—Armadillo, Sidney, and Flip-Lip. But here's another mystery. Why are the three henchmen dressed like hotel cleaning ladies? Let's listen and see if we can find out.

"What a scheme, Perfesser!" Sidney is saying.

"Yeah!" says Armadillo. "While you drive this submarine around the lake and get all the hotel guests out of their rooms, we rob 'em!"

"Here's the loot we got this morning, Professor," Armadillo says, dumping a sack of stolen goods onto the table.

"What's this?" the Professor says, picking up Sleuth's Stradivarius violin. "A fiddle? Where's the bow?"

"We'll get it tomorrow," says Flip-Lip.

Back at the hotel Sleuth was looking at the pictures he had taken of the monster. He handed Mickey a pile of snapshots.

"Not now, Sleuth," Mickey said, deep in thought. "I'm trying to figure out. . . . Wait a minute! Let me see those pictures!" Mickey looked closely at one of Sleuth's pictures. "What's *this*?"

"It's a porthole," Sleuth replied. "I didn't know monsters had portholes."

"Neither did I!" Mickey said, heading for the door. "I'll be back in a little while. I'm going to take a look around the bottom of that lake. There's something fishy going on down there!"

Mickey rowed out to the middle of the lake. After putting on his diving goggles and flippers, he made sure the air tank on his back was working. Then, with a splash, he dived over the side of the rowboat and into the lake.

Mickey swam downward until he could see the sandy bottom. Suddenly, a large, dark shape loomed up in front of him. The Loch Ness Monster! No. Wait a minute. It wasn't a monster. It was a . . . *submarine!*

"Just as I suspected," Mickey thought.

The sub gurgled by. Mickey got a quick look through the porthole. At the controls of the underwater boat stood a familiar figure—Professor Nefarious!

The sub was heading toward the shore at the far end of the lake. Mickey followed. The sub came to a spot hidden from the hotel by trees and bushes. There it surfaced. Watching from behind a rock, Mickey saw the submarine hatch open. Three cleaning ladies hopped out and jumped ashore.

A few minutes later, the "monster" popped its head out of the middle of the lake. Once again, all the hotel guests dashed out of their rooms. They ran to the edge of the lake.

"Oops!" Sleuth said. "I forgot my camera." He turned away from the lake and ran back to the hotel.

The three "cleaning ladies" were pulling apart Sleuth's room, looking for the violin bow. Suddenly, Sleuth was in the doorway. When he saw what a mess the room was, he became furious. "You call yourselves *cleaning* ladies?" he fumed.

"Just look at this mess! Come along with me. I'm reporting this to the manager!"

Sleuth marched the three downstairs and out the front door. The manager was down by the lake with everybody else. They were staring at a funny-looking submarine. And there was Mickey, standing on its deck.

Back in London, Sleuth was reading the morning paper. From across the breakfast table, Mickey saw the headline—

SLEUTH SOLVES LOCH NESS MONSTER HOAX!

"I see they've mentioned *your* name here on page twenty-six, Mickey," Sleuth said. "It's only fair. After all, you *did* help me!"

"Nice of you to say so, Sleuth," Mickey replied. "Too bad the Professor got away. But when I captured his sub, I had to take over the controls. I was so busy, the Professor got out of one of the escape hatches before I could stop him. But you did a fine job catching the rest of the gang."

Sleuth nodded. "If I hadn't remembered I forgot my camera, I never would have captured them. Our vacation did wonders for my memory."

"That's a nice picture of you in the paper," Mickey said.

"Is *that* who it is?" Sleuth said. "I've been wondering where I've seen that face before!"